This princess book belongs to

....

☆

Koori Princess

This is a Magabala Book
LEADING PUBLISHER OF ABORIGINAL AND
TORRES STRAIT ISLANDER STORYTELLERS.
CHANGING THE WORLD, ONE STORY AT A TIME.

First published 2022
Magabala Books Aboriginal Corporation
1 Bagot Street, Broome, Western Australia
Website: www.magabala.com
Email: sales@magabala.com

Magabala Books receives financial assistance from the Commonwealth Government through the Australia Council, its arts advisory body. The State of Western Australia has made an investment in this project through the Department of Local Government, Sport and Cultural Industries. Magabala Books would like to acknowledge the support of the Shire of Broome, Western Australia.

Magabala Books is Australia's only independent Aboriginal and Torres Strait Islander publishing house. Magabala Books acknowledges the Traditional Owners of the Country on which we live and work. We recognise the unbroken connection to traditional lands, waters and cultures. Through what we publish, we honour all our Elders, peoples and stories, past, present and future.

Cover design Gene Eaton, Magabala Books
Cover image & illustrations Samantha Campbell
Typeset by Post Pre-press Group
Printed and bound by Griffin Press, South Australia
Author photo by Kate Bryan (Ruby Olive)

ISBN (Print) 978-1-922613-15-8
ISBN (ePDF) 978-1-922613-16-5
ISBN (ePub) 978-1-875641-11-6

A catalogue record for this book is available from the National Library of Australia

Department of Local Government, Sport and Cultural Industries
Australian Government
Australia Council for the Arts
Shire of Broome

Koori Princess

Anita Heiss

Magabala Books

For all the Koori princesses out there,
follow your dreams.

ONE
I'm a princess

'Teish, time for schoooool,' Helen calls to her daughter for the third time. But the soon-to-be eight-year-old continues to sit grinning at the screen, not moving, not hearing anything other than the words of a tune from the animated movie she is watching.

'Teish, I won't call you again!'

There is still no movement from Teish whose eyes and ears remain glued to the television.

'Can you please get your daughter away from the TV, into her uniform and off to school?'

Helen asks her husband with a hint of frustration in her voice. 'Honestly, I'm losing my patience.'

Jamie walks to the loungeroom, pokes his head around the doorway and softly says, 'Princess, come on, it's time for school.'

Teish gets up without taking her eyes off the movie and walks backwards towards the door, mumbling 'Okay' as she presses the button on the remote and watches the colourful screen turn black.

'Your eyes will turn square sitting that close to the television, you know that don't you?' Jamie says as his daughter pirouettes her way past him, giggling as she spins down the hallway to her bedroom.

When Jamie enters the kitchen whistling, Helen shakes her head. 'Why does she listen to you and not me when I ask her to get ready for school?'

'Because I use that magic word,' he nods and winks.

As Jamie sits down to toast and tea, his eldest daughter Karan walks into the kitchen, perfectly groomed with her head in a maths book. She is quickly followed by her elder brother Kim and cousin Ruby, who are passing a football back and forth across the room.

'How many times do I have to tell you?' Helen pauses but there is no response. 'No balls in the house,' she says without looking up, rushing to pack their lunches like a production line before she leaves for work.

Karan picks up a pile of invitations from the breakfast bar. 'What are these?'

Helen spins around, ready to defend herself from a barrage of questions. She grabs the envelopes from Karan and puts them in Teish's backpack.

'They're the invitations to your sister's birthday party.'

Karan rolls her eyes. 'What's this year's theme? Oh no, let me guess,' she looks into the distance, pretending to ponder the possibilities. Sarcastically she asks, 'Is it ... could it possibly be ... a princess party?'

'DO NOT say *anything* to your sister about her party. You know she loves the princess movies.'

Helen gives the order with a strong stare. 'Do you hear me?' She waits for a nod of acknowledgement, which eventually comes but is quickly followed by a comment.

'Mum! It's not watching the movies that's the problem, it's that she actually *thinks* she *is* a princess!'

'Don't be silly. She's just a bit of a dreamer.'

'She's a daydream believer,' Jamie sings the tune of an old song that makes both adults in the room smile and Karan roll her eyes again.

'Don't roll your eyes,' Jamie says without turning around, and Karan frowns. 'Or frown. You know I have eyes in the back of my head and I see e-v-e-r-y-t-h-i-n-g!'

'Karan, you've always found inspiration and ideas from watching movies too, don't forget that,' Helen reminds her daughter.

'I have not!' Karan says adamantly.

'Have you forgotten your dream to be an aeronautical engineer came from learning about Mary Jackson in that movie you watched, what was it?'

'Hidden Figures,' Jamie says, turning a page of the newspaper.

'Mum, please. Being inspired by watching a film about women helping put men into space is *completely* different to watching a cartoon about waiting for a prince to rescue you so you can live happily ever after in a castle.'

'Ah but what about the detective heroine you loved from that Hollywood movie? Even *she* ended up with her prince in the end.'

'Sandra Bullock in Miss Congeniality,' Jamie adds.

'Oh yes, she ended up with the dreamboat Benjamin Bratt,' Ruby hugs the football.

'You're not helping,' Karan glares at Ruby. 'And what's your point, Mum?'

'You've forgotten that when you were a little girl you wanted to be a policewoman after you watched that movie.'

A look of recognition flashes across Karan's face and her mother smiles.

'That's right, isn't it? A policewoman who rode a motorbike. But your father pointed out that you were a bit too short and your feet wouldn't touch the ground.'

'That's right,' Jamie pipes in. 'So you decided to be a policewoman on a horse instead because you could adjust the stirrups to meet your feet.'

'That was clever thinking, Sis,' Kim is impressed.

'Maybe that's when you started loving maths and measurements,' Ruby adds.

'But now you don't want to be a policewoman, you want to be an engineer instead. And your father and I really don't care what you want to be as long as you work hard and you're happy. Know you're smart and you can do anything you put your mind to.'

'Yeah, you're the smart cousin,' Ruby tosses the football in the air. 'And I'm the sporty one.'

'And what about you, Ruby?' Helen asks her niece, taking the ball from her and placing it under a nearby stool.

'What about me, Aunty Helen?' Ruby sounds concerned.

'You wanted to be a vet when you were little, Rubes. You always loved animals and you were always rescuing animals.'

'Yeah, you were always bringing home stray cats and wanting to make them well before they even got sick,' Jamie adds.

'It's true, I did. I was such a good kid, eh?'

'Yes, you were, but let's be honest, you haven't mentioned being a vet for years,' Helen says.

'Umm, I know but I am a vegan now because I don't want to eat animals, so doesn't that count for something?'

'Of course it does, and it's admirable,' Jamie pipes in. 'But you don't even walk Shandy with me after school.'

'I know, I'm sorry, I have training most days after school.' Ruby looks at the ball, willing it to roll out from under that chair.

Helen looks to her niece. 'Football is all you ever talk about these days.'

'And what's wrong with that?' Karan asks.

'There's absolutely nothing wrong with it, Karan.'

'Then *again* Mum, what's your point?' Karan sounds impatient.

'Excuse me?' Helen waves a dishcloth at Karan

and flicks water all over the place. 'Firstly, lose that tone young lady and don't question me like you're a lawyer and I am a criminal. I am your mother. And secondly, before you roll your eyes again, just don't. My point is that what we dream of being as children or even in our teens and twenties is not always, if ever, what we end up doing with our lives in the years and decades that follow.'

'But *you* did. You said you always wanted to be a nurse, even as a child, and now you are the best nurse this side of the Great Dividing Range, as Dad always says.'

Everyone looks to the patriarch, who nods his agreement.

'Yes, I did. And when I was your sister's age, I dressed up in a nurse's outfit with a toy thermometer and a stethoscope. I had a red plastic medicine bag and I dreamed of saving lives. I bandaged my bears and your uncles and aunts' arms and ankles.'

'I bet you were really cute in that nurse's uniform too,' Jamie says and the teenagers all groan in unison.

'Dad!'

'Uncle! Yuk!'

'Okay, okay, I get it, you can dream and change, it's true. But it's not the same with Teish. You can't deny that she lives in a fantasy world most of the time, and that can't be healthy.' Karan bites into a piece of toast.

'Karan, fantasy and imagination are good for children. I want you *all* to be creative thinkers, to imagine worlds outside of this one.'

'What? Like Disney World?' Kim butts in and urges Ruby to grab the ball from under the stool and pass it his way.

'No, like you imagine your life as a pro surfer and Karan imagines hers at university, being an engineer, being a professor or being whatever she wants.'

'Dreaming of being a professor is not the same as believing you're a princess, Mum,' Karan rolls her eyes again.

Helen hands Karan her lunch bag. 'All I want is for you all to be happy. Teish is young, it's important to let her be an individual. And she is the happiest kid I know.'

'And don't roll your eyes at your mother,' Jamie says.

'How do you even see me?'

'I told you, I have eyes in the back of my head.'

Karan puts her fingers to her eyes, as if to keep them from rolling into the back of her skull.

'Aunt, I totally agree that it's good to think outside the box,' Ruby says, 'that's why I'm going to be a star AFL player in the women's league. But even I knew by Teish's age that life wasn't like a Disney movie. And that no Prince Charming was going to turn up in a chariot to save me or make my life complete.'

Kim grabs the ball himself and tosses it to Ruby while his mother has her back to them. 'Well, no bloke at all is going to turn up if you dress and play footy like a fella!'

'Don't talk stupid, Cuz! Any bloke interested in me will be into footy and think it's deadly that I'm in the A-league. And that I can kick a goal like Erin Phillips.'

'You're dreaming!'

'Lucky I don't want to play rugby league 'cause I'd tackle you to the ground right here, right now.'

'Yeah, tackling, that'd attract your prince for sure,' Kim laughs.

'I'm not even looking for a prince Cuz, just a decent deadly fella to carry my footy gear to games for me so I can focus.'

Kim shakes his head as he catches the ball then tosses it back and forth between his hands. 'Mum, I'm sorry but I'm siding with these two today,' he says, nodding to Karan and Ruby. 'Do you really think it's okay for Teish to be obsessed with being a princess? I mean, not only is she turning eight soon, but ...' Kim pauses cautiously.

'But what?' Helen sounds tired of this conversation about her daughter's love of fairytales.

'Well, I hate to be the one to say it out loud, because she *is* my sister.'

Jamie cuts him off. 'Then don't say it.'

'But the thing is,' Kim pauses again, 'she's a bit chubby to be a princess, don't you think?'

'KIM!' Jamie, Helen, Karan and Ruby sing out in shocked unison.

Jamie stands up, both hands on the kitchen table, and Kim knows he may be in big trouble.

'Do not *ever* say anything like that to Teish, ever! Do you hear me?'

'Yes, sir.'

Karan adds, seething, 'To *any* girl *or* woman. *Ever*!'

'EVER!' Ruby's eyes are bulging so much it looks like her head might explode with fury over Kim's ignorance.

'All right, but what's the big deal? She *is* chubby, probably because she sits inside watching those stupid movies instead of playing outside. Is there a fat princess she's a fan of? 'Cause that dream might just come true for her.'

'You need help!' Ruby says, shaking her head.

'Fat shaming, making fun of someone being overweight,' Karan says through gritted teeth. 'And she is your baby sister, you should be building up her self-esteem, not smashing it into pieces.'

'Only someone worried about their own body image comments or makes fun of someone else's.' Ruby is disgusted.

'Stop overreacting, I wasn't making fun, I was just stating facts.'

'Don't gaslight me, and stop with your alternative facts. Next you'll be quoting Trump.'

'Don't be such feminazis.'

Karan and Ruby stand side by side, arms linked, sisters-in-arms. 'Do *not* liken us being strong Koori women with goals to something as disgusting and repulsive as the holocaust.' Karan's blood is boiling.

Ruby is equally shocked and angry. 'What is wrong with you? The holocaust was awful beyond words.'

'I wasn't comparing you to the holocaust. A feminazi is—'

'DO NOT boy-splain things to me, Brother!'

'Or me!' Ruby snatches the ball from Kim then starts laughing a hard belly laugh. Karan joins in.

Kim is confused. 'What's so funny?'

'I bet you don't even know how to *spell* feminazi,' Ruby scoffs, laughing harder. Karan slaps her on the back.

'He can barely spell his own name and there's only one syllable. Hang on,' Karan takes a breath, 'do you know what a syllable is?' The two cousins laugh some more.

'Oh right, so it's okay for you to be offensive and rude to me now, is it?' Kim sounds wounded as Teish enters the kitchen and silence falls over all of them.

'Okay that's enough you mob, your mum needs to get to the hospital and I need to get to work. Who wants a ride to school? I'm taking Princess and there's room for one more in the cabin of the truck.'

Karan, Ruby and Kim look at each other and shake their heads. 'We'll get the bus, thanks Dad,' Karan responds.

As Jamie and Teish walk out of the house, Kim says quietly, 'It's *his* fault, calling her Princess all the time.'

Helen catches her son and pushes his lunch into his hands, half laughing, half cranky, knowing that her husband *is* partly responsible for Teish believing she is a princess.

*

Teish is crying uncontrollably as Helen sits on the bed rubbing her back. Her daughter is howling to the point she almost turns blue when she breathes in to let out another mighty 'WAAAHHHH!'

Jamie races into the room concerned. 'What's going on in here?' He looks to his daughter then to his wife. 'I heard you crying from the garage when I pulled in.'

Kim appears next to his father. 'The neighbours can hear you, they're all out the front having a durrie.'

'Stop it,' Helen frowns at Kim.

'Well, who died then?'

Teish springs upright. 'My party died!' She lets out another 'WAAAHHHH!' as she collapses back onto the bed.

Kim slaps his forehead. 'Unbelievable, alert the press.'

'Can you please go and do something useful Kim, like your homework?' Helen says.

He turns and walks out the door mumbling, 'She really is too much.'

'What happened?' Jamie asks.

'A couple of the parents rang to say their girls wouldn't come as princesses to Teish's party. In fact, they didn't want their girls to come at all.'

Jamie shrugs and frowns, mouthing 'Why?'

Helen strokes Teish's hair as she moves her head to the comfort of her mother's lap.

'Mandy's mother said all those princess films are for white girls, that we should decolonise our minds and not buy into all that ...' she pauses, looking for the right word to say in front of her youngest. 'All that bulldust,' her eyes widen so that Jamie knows exactly what word was said.

Teish suddenly springs upright again. 'It wasn't just Mandy's mum, it was Belinda's and Lou's parents too.' She collapses back into her mother's lap and continues to bawl. 'They all hate me.'

'No-one hates you, it has nothing to do with you, Teish.' Helen takes her daughter's hand in her own. 'But they are right, you know, those princess movies do lack diversity, and they do suggest a lot about how girls and women should live, and it's not the way we live or the way we want you to think about your life.'

Teish sobs and sniffles, lost in her own misery. 'They all hate me, and I hate them back.'

Helen shakes her head, knowing her daughter is dramatic at the best of times, and hopes this will all blow over soon. Right now, though, she has a very unhappy princess on her hands.

'What should we do?' Helen asks.

'Maybe we can change the theme of the party?' Jamie suggests.

'WAAAHHHHH,' comes another outburst from Teish.

'I don't know, they've raised valid points,' Helen says. 'The original films lack diversity and are overdone with stereotypes. It's hard for people of colour to relate to the stories and why should we?'

'But aren't a lot of the films different now? I'm sure I've seen brown princesses on the screen,' Jamie says. 'I probably should take more interest in what she's watching on TV.'

Helen nods in agreement as Teish springs upright, wiping her nose on her sleeve. 'Moana is a Polynesian princess, she's brown.' She flops down again.

Jamie and Helen look at each other and shrug their shoulders simultaneously.

Teish bolts up again. 'Elena of Avalor is brown, she's a Latina princess,' she says, flopping down once more only to spring back up immediately. She doesn't open her eyes when she adds, "That's a woman from Latin America, in case you didn't know.'

Jamie can't help but smile at how clever his little princess is.

'And Pocahontas is brown, she's like Aboriginal in America.' Teish takes a deep breath and looks strangely excited. 'And my favourite, Tiana, she is a beautiful Black princess from the deep south of America.'

'You're right, Teish,' Jamie kisses his daughter on the head.

'And *I* am Princess Teish, a beautiful Koori princess.'

'Yes, you are. But ...'

'But what?'

'You *are* beautiful and you are your *dad's* princess, but Teish, you need to understand that in our stories over time, we did not have princesses,' Jamie explains.

'And there is no word in our language for princess,' Helen adds. 'We have a lot of different words for women and girls, and we are all very special in our own ways, but no-one is better than anyone else.'

'I know that I am not better than anyone else.'

'Good, because we must always remember we are equal and we must treat people as our equals,' Jamie says. 'But in history and even today, a princess is part of a royal family that has households and kingdoms with servants and riches that normal people like us would never have, even if we wanted them.'

'Don't you want to be rich?' Teish is surprised to think that her parents don't want buckets of gold and a big, fancy house.

'Your mum and I are rich in love and all that you kids bring into our lives. That's the kind of riches we want. And we work hard to earn money to buy some of the things that we also like to have.'

'Like our pool and car?'

'That's exactly right.'

'But to be a real princess, not just a daddy's princess, you are born into that role or you marry into a family that is already a royal family. And people who are royal don't really ever marry people who aren't already royal too.'

'But Harry and Meghan did.'

'Yes, they did.'

'And Frederik married Mary and she was just a girl from Tasmania.'

'Yes, she was.'

'Oh boy, we are losing this argument,' Helen chuckles. 'Teish, we just want you to understand that being a princess is fine to dream about as a young girl, but it is not a job you can apply for.'

'Okay,' Teish sniffles and shrugs her shoulders as if in defeat.

'What we're trying to say is that princesses are part of families that are part of a society where there is a very strong hierarchy, with a class system that would have *our* family—you and me and your dad—near the bottom of that system. But *our* ways, *our* values and society mean *everyone* is equal, that all our roles are important. And that's why we don't have princesses or princes with servants and subjects.'

Teish looks into her mother's eyes, searching for more information, then, as if it suddenly becomes clear, she says, 'I guess that makes sense.'

TWO

Sandcastles, bluebottle stings and little mermaids

'See ya, wouldn't want to be ya!' Kim takes off towards the surf as the sun sits high in the sky.

'Have you got sunscreen on?' Karan yells after him. 'Honestly, I feel like his mother sometimes.'

'He thinks he is so hot, true god, believes all the girls at school love him,' Ruby says, rubbing lotion all over her body. 'At least one of us won't be getting melanoma this year. Can you put some on the back of my neck please, Cuz?' she asks, turning her back to Karan while zipping up her rashie. 'I'm covering all bases, you know, Kooris can get sun cancer too, eh?'

'What about me? Koori princesses need lotion too,' Teish says, strutting over to her big sister. 'Do you like my Moana bikini? I got it for Christmas.' She spins around three times, then stumbles from being dizzy. 'Woah,' she says, hitting the sand and giggling. Ruby and Karan can't help but laugh too.

'Come here, you crazy kid,' Ruby helps Teish up, dusts the sand off her and rubs lots of lotion all over her arms and legs.

'Moana means ocean, did you know that?' Teish says as she turns to get lotion on her back. 'That's why it's good to wear this to the beach.' Teish strikes a pose and the older girls laugh again at the strong sense of self-esteem Teish has.

'You *are* cute, come here,' Karan says. 'Put this hat on or you'll end up with more freckles than a leopard has spots.'

Teish sees her brother's friends Marc and Joe walking towards them with boards under their arms. She has a sparkle in her eye when Marc waves to her.

'Here comes Marc,' she says, grinning widely.

'Hi there,' Marc says, 'where's the Golden Boy?' He looks up and down the length of the beach, and Teish watches him, eyes twinkling.

Joe looks out to the surf. 'There he is, can't miss that manbun. True god, he thinks he is Jason Momoa.'

'He wishes,' Ruby says, getting ready to surf herself.

'You going in today, Ruby?' Marc asks.

'Ummm, well, I *am* putting a leg-rope on, so what do you think?'

Marc feels deflated. He wishes Ruby was a little less sarcastic and kinder to him. He doesn't understand how she can't see he fancies her.

'I'm going in too, in my Moana cozzie.' Teish strikes a pose, hoping to take Marc's attention from her cousin.

'Oh, for goodness sake, stop with Moana already.' Karan picks up a plastic bucket and spade. 'Let's make a sandcastle.'

'Great idea, a sandcastle for beach princesses, you are really smart, Sissy.'

Karan shakes her head at her own mistake in mentioning the word 'castle' in front of her sister.

'I can help if you like, Karan?' Joe offers, waiting for an opportunity to be close to Karan and not hiding his crush very well.

'Whatever!' Karan pretends she doesn't see the way Joe looks at her.

'Come,' Teish takes Joe's hand, having forgotten Marc quickly, and skips him down to the water's edge.

'Come on then, can't have Kim getting all the good waves, eh?' Ruby heads to the water with Marc in tow and they run into the surf, pushing their boards over the whitewash and into the waves.

On the shoreline Joe and Teish fill buckets of sea water and start building their sandcastle.

'Oh, this will be one grand palace, Teish.

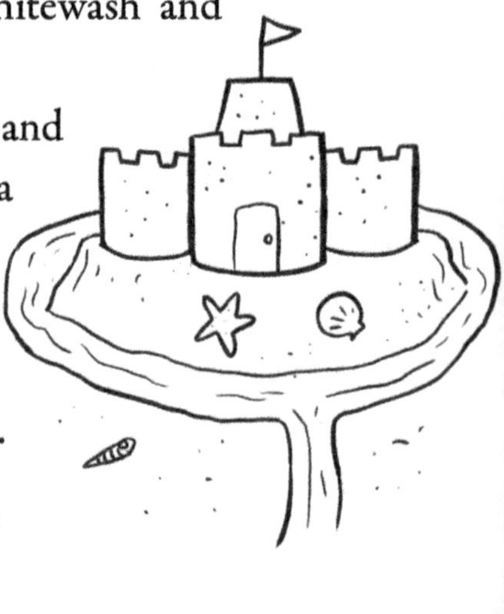

Let's build rooms for all of us, and our families and friends.'

'That's a great idea. Are you going to be a builder one day?'

'No, I'm going to be a comedian.'

'What's a comedian do?'

'They tell jokes, make people laugh, because they are very, very funny.'

'Are you very, very funny?' Teish asks innocently.

'Well, let's see,' Joe dusts the sand off his hands, stands up and holds the spade as if it is a microphone.

'What did the ocean say to the pirate?'

Teish shrugs, 'What?'

'Nothing, it just *waved*.'

'That's funny!' Teish giggles while Karan groans and rolls her eyes.

'Thank you very much, you're a deadly audience.'

'Tell another one.'

'Okay, why did the crab cross the beach?'

'Why?' Teish asks, wide-eyed.

'To get to the other *tide*.'

Karan rolls her eyes again and Teish laughs out loud. 'Got another one?'

'This one is a special one just for you Teish, because you are the best audience member ever.'

'Okay, go!'

'What does Cinderella wear at the beach?'

Teish strains to think of something funny but can't. She finally shrugs her shoulders. 'I give up. What does Cinderella wear at the beach?'

'Glass *flippers*!' Joe slaps his thigh at his own humour. Teish claps and Karan rolls her eyes and shakes her head.

'You know you really should stop doing that,' Joe says as he tips a bucket of sand over to build another tower in their castle.

'Doing what?'

'That eyerolling.'

'Don't *you* start, Mum and Dad are bad enough.'

'I'm just saying, you do it a lot.'

'I do not.'

'Umm, yes you do. You just did it three times in front of me.'

'You did too, Sis. I saw you.'

'And,' Joe pauses. He doesn't want to upset Karan or get her angry because he wants to ask her to his school formal, but he can see her standing there waiting impatiently.

'And what?'

'Well, it's a bit rude to do that once, let alone three times to the same person who is just trying to make a little girl smile.'

Teish looks up to Joe. 'And you did, you made me laugh because you are a very, very funny person.'

'Be quiet, both of you,' Karan snaps.

'Okay,' Joe concedes that the conversation has ended, so stops talking and starts whistling as he and Teish continue to work on the castle, fashioning a moat around it to catch the surf that reaches them.

'What if, just say, I *did, hypothetically,* roll my eyes, *occasionally.* What would be the impact of that?'

'Well, apart from the fact that I've heard it can give you headaches, it could, hypothetically, offend people because it's really saying something sarcastic with your eyes.'

'Yeah, I know,' Karan mumbles.

'But that's not the only thing.'

'Oh, don't stop now, go on, please, tell me what else I'm doing wrong, please.' Karan just stops herself from yet another eyeroll. And before Joe says anything she says, 'I know, I know, go on.'

'You see Karan, the thing is that *I* know that you roll your eyes when you are annoyed or maybe even bored—usually at me, or someone else you like,' he smiles, 'but other people might think it means something else.'

'Like what? I'm sure you make half this stuff up.' Karan sounds annoyed but her eyes are still.

'Well, I won't tell you then,' Joe says, building another tower in the sandcastle.

'Oh, go on, you know you want to, just give it to me.'

'Well, back in the old days, like when our grandparents were born, eyerolling was a form of flirting.'

'You are full of it.'

'You can choose to believe me or not, but that's what I read somewhere, probably on Facewaste.'

'It can't mean *that*. As if eyerolling is flirting. That idea alone makes me want to roll my eyes!'

'Don't shoot the messenger, so to speak. But you might want to consider that signature eyeroll of yours, as *some* people, some young man for example, might get the wrong idea about what you are trying to say.' Joe winks at Karan, who looks panicked.

'No way,' she says, throwing her plastic shovel down.

'Yes way.' Joe chuckles hard, which makes Teish laugh too.

'Well, rest assured I am not flirting with *anyone* when I roll my eyes.'

'I know that because it also makes your face look ...'

'Look what?' Karan demands.

'Look not as pretty as it is when your eyes are normal.'

Karan squints at Joe. 'And are *you* flirting with *me* now? 'Cause if you are, *don't*!'

'No, I'm not flirting, I just didn't want to say that you look constipated when you do that.'

Karan gasps but before she can say anything, Teish is asking questions.

'What's flirting?' Teish asks as she tips some water from her bucket into the freshly finished moat. 'And what's constipated?'

'You started this,' Karan points to Joe laughing, 'you finish it.'

'I'm a bloke! It's not my place to tell a young girl what flirting is.'

'Well, if you're going to be into such gender roles then you'll never need to worry about a girl flirting with you because she won't!'

'Okay, okay, I get it.' Joe turns to Teish. 'When someone likes someone else, they sometimes behave a certain way, and that is called flirting.'

'Oh, that is genius, you said absolutely nothing then.'

Teish ignores Karan and stands up and says to Joe while dusting sand from her knees, 'Kind of like when you and Karan make fun of each other but it's only playing, because you want to be boyfriend and girlfriend but don't want to say it out loud?'

'What? No, no way.' Karan disagrees strongly. 'And for the record, I hope your actual flirting is better than your explanation of it.'

Joe is deflated but hides his feelings well. 'I hope so too!'

They are both grateful for the sound of Marc yelling from the surf. A painful, loud yell that has everyone on the shoreline looking in his direction as he limps from the water with Ruby and Kim on either side of him.

'What's going on?' Karan races to them concerned.

'I've been stung! I've been stung by a bluebottle.'

'Where?'

'My foot, my foot.'

When he reaches the dry sand and finally collapses onto his bum, they can all see that the bluebottle is still wrapped around his foot.

'Get it off, get it off,' Marc screams.

'Calm down, calm down,' Ruby urges as she gets in close.

A tear forms in Marc's left eye and Kim jumps at the opportunity to have a dig. 'You're not crying like a girl, are you? Man up Brother, man up.'

'Back off Kim, have you ever been stung by a bluey? I can tell you the pain is excruciating,' Ruby says angrily. 'And stop with the "crying like a girl" crap or I'll try my three new kickboxing moves on you, like a girl.' Ruby does her best to demonstrate on the sand.

'Oh god, the pain, where's the lifesavers? The stretcher?'

Even Ruby tries not to laugh at the request for a stretcher.

'You don't need a lifesaver, your life doesn't need to be saved,' Kim says and then turns to Karan. 'And what are you doing, instagramming? Yeah, get the tears in the photo, everyone at school will want to see that for sure.'

'You really are a boofhead sometimes. I'm googling how to cure a bluebottle sting.' She looks at her phone and reads out a list. 'Wash area with sea water and remove any tentacles. Run hot water on it for twenty minutes.'

Kim butts in, 'Well, we can't do that, can we?'

'OR you can let me finish,' Karan glares at him. 'Put an ice pack on it.' She turns and points to the esky. 'Teish, grab one of your frozen juice packs out of the esky, we can use that.'

Joe holds his phone to Karan. 'What I'm reading says you can pee on a bluey sting.'

'Yuk!' Teish screws her face up as she rummages through the esky then hands the juice box to Karan, who places it on Marc's foot.

'No-one is peeing on my foot! I don't care how much this hurts. That's a myth anyway, keep reading.'

Joe is laughing.

'What's so funny?'

'I knew it was a myth but love the look on your face. Priceless.'

'I'm so glad you can find humour in my pain.'

'They don't call me Joe the Joker for no reason.'

'Joe is really funny,' Teish announces. 'Can you come to my party and make my friends laugh too?'

'That I can. Do you think your big sister will be back to eyerolling? That might make your friends laugh too, like a party trick.'

'Hardy har har,' Karan says.

'I think she liked me better before,' Joe whispers to Teish.

'I think you're right, and I think she *was* flirting with you, Joe the Joker.'

THREE

The princess party

'It's my birthday, it's my birthday!' Teish runs through the house in a frenzy, excited about her party which is only hours away.

'Princesses probably don't run and screech like that, Teish!' Helen sings out after the birthday girl as she and Karan fill princess-themed lolly bags for the guests.

'Mum, Teish can't be doing this for her next birthday, surely,' Karan waves a princess serviette in the air. 'She is getting too old for this fairytale nonsense.'

'You're never too old, Karan,' Helen responds defensively. 'I love watching the movies with your sister, your father even watches sometimes.'

'Yes, but you and Dad know the difference between reality and fiction, real life and fairytales.'

'And your little sister will know the difference soon enough too. Why rob her of the joy a simple movie brings her? And it's her *birthday*! Isn't she the happiest person you know?'

Karan smiles, watching her sister help their father hang streamers in the backyard.

'Yes, she really is a bundle of joy, when she's not screaming the street down with tears.' They both laugh.

'As long as she's not expecting her Prince Charming to come and rescue her. Because for as long as I can remember you've told Ruby and me not to wait for any man to make our lives complete. That we are responsible for our own happiness, for our own completeness.'

'And it's true.'

'What's true?' Jamie asks, grabbing a lolly from the production line.

'That your daughters, including your Princess Teish out there,' they all look out the window to see Teish weaving pink streamers through the lemon tree, 'should not be waiting around for a Prince Charming to fulfil their lives.'

'Of course not, no fella is ever going to be good enough for my girls anyway.' He grabs another lolly while Karan rolls her eyes.

'I saw that eyeroll Daught, you need to stop doing that,' he winks. ''Cause you know that show of contempt will scare not only the fellas off, but pretty much everyone else too.'

'Yeah, so I've been told,' Karan mumbles under her breath.

'Also, it must be said that I am *still* your mother's knight in shining armour.' Jamie pulls Helen close and kisses her on the cheek.

'Knight in a blue singlet is more like it,' Helen says, laughing.

'Okay I'm ready to ice the cake now, Mum. It should be cool enough.' Teish has snuck into the kitchen and quickly tied her apron over her party dress.

'Pink butter frosting like we discussed, with these pink flowers Bec from next door gave me. She said they are nasty-umms.'

'Nasturtiums,' Helen says. 'They're nasturtiums.'

Teish frowns, 'That's what I said, Mum. Anyway, Bec had mostly yellow nasty-umms but I took the pink ones 'cause that's my favourite colour. You can eat them.' She pops one in her mouth and then arranges the rest on the counter.

Over the next while Teish whips the frosting, dropping pink food colouring into the buttery mix until it is the perfect colour and consistency. She and her mother also make some vegan cookies for Ruby and her friends who don't eat anything that has animal products in it.

'I love baking with you, Mum.'

'And *I* love baking with you, Daught.'

'Do you think I could own a bakery one day?' Teish licks the beater.

'I think you can do whatever you put your mind to, but I don't think you can lick beaters in a business where you serve food to the public.' Helen takes a wooden spoon from the cookie mix and licks it. 'But here at home, well, that's a different story.' She takes one more lick and puts the spoon in the sink.

*

'Happy birthday dear Teeeeeiiish, happy birthday to yoooooou! Hip, hip, hooray! Hip, hip, hooray!'

Teish takes a huge breath and leans in to blow out the eight candles on the princess cake her mother has made for her. There's cheering and giggling as the guests stand waiting to taste the pink cream creation.

'I don't think you should have cake,' Teish says to Kim.

'Huh, why? I love princess cake!' He winks to Karan and Ruby.

'But you ate all the fairy bread, so I think you might like fairies better than princesses.'

'I don't like anything more than my little sister. Now where's my cake?'

'Right here,' Teish giggles as she pulls from behind her back a paper plate with Kim's piece of cake on it, nearly tipping it over before he catches it.

'That's more like it, thanks Sis.'

'Who wants to skip?' Ruby walks through the cake-eating crowd to the driveway. 'Come on Golden Boy, you can turn one end.' Kim shoves his cake in his mouth and swallows without chewing.

The rope turns slowly and all the princesses line up to jump.

'Me first,' Teish pushes to the front with the support and enthusiasm of all the other kids. She moves her hands in time with the rope as it goes around and round and round, one, two, three.

'Come on, you'll be ten years old if you don't hurry up!' Kim says.

One, two, three she counts in her head and then runs into the centre of the turning rope. She skips the rope four times before she starts singing,

'Cinderella dressed in yella
Went upstairs to kiss her fella
How many kisses did she give him?'

And they all start counting together, 'One, two, three, four, five, six …'

Teish stops and another voice sings out.

'Cinderella dressed in yella
Went upstairs to kiss her fella
By mistake she kissed a snake
How many doctors will it take?'

'One, two, three, four—'

'No! No! No!' Ruby says, dropping the rope. 'Let me tell you what the words should be. Karan, can you turn it while I jump?'

Karan picks up the rope. She and Marc start turning it super fast and the younger girls clap and cheer as Ruby lines up the rope like she is lining up to kick a goal. When she runs into the centre she starts singing straight away.

'Cinderella in red, black and yella
Went to the footy to meet a fella
When she got there

She didn't care
'Cause she kicked a goal and that was stellar
How many goals did she kick?'

'One, two, three, four, five, six, seven, eight!'

'Wow, you're the queen of skipping!' Teish says. 'But I think we need to get out of the sun now.' She turns and sings out to Joe standing nearby watching. 'Joe the Joker, can you make my friends laugh please?'

'Absolutely!' He responds and starts to walk. 'Let's all sit under the tree just over here.' When all the kids are seated he takes a wand from one of the princesses and pretends it is a microphone. 'Are you ready?'

'YEESSSSS!' comes the communal response.

Joe looks at them all and asks the question slowly, 'What one thing will you get every year on your birthday, guaranteed?'

'Presents.'

'Cake.'

'A party,' come the responses.

'A year older!' he yells and laughs so hard the kids laugh with him.

'Okay, what do you say to a rabbit on its birthday?' and before anyone sings out he yells, 'Hoppy Birthday!' Everyone laughs again, and Karan notices how good Joe is with the young ones.

'Wait, there's more,' Joe says and the kids sit upright, ready for the next joke. 'What did the cake say to the ice-cream?' He takes a deep breath. 'You're cool!'

Once the laughter dies down he turns to Teish, smiles and bows.

'And finally, to the birthday girl. Teish, are you ready?'

Teish nods with anticipation in her eyes.

'Knock, knock,' Joe asks.

'Who's there?' Teish giggles.

'Wanda.'

'Wanda who?'

'Wanda wish you a happy birthday!'

Joe picks up his best mate's sister and spins her around, singing 'Happy birthday!'

FOUR

Aladdin

'I can't believe we have to review this rubbish!' Kim turns on the television as Marc and Joe get settled on the lounge.

'I think it's cool to get to review a film that's been popular for twenty years,' Marc says. 'It's like, ancient!'

'Popular with girls like Teish, you mean.'

'Did I hear my name?' Teish pops her head sheepishly around the corner, spots Marc and then lunges right into the room, smiling at the cutest boy she knows.

'Not now, Teish. We have homework to do.'

'What is it?' she asks, smiling at Marc.

'We have to watch Aladdin and write a review of it.'

'Oh, I love Aladdin and Princess Jasmine, I can tell you all about it. I've watched it a gazillion times.'

'Not now, Teish!' Kim raises his voice and Teish's bottom lip drops and begins to quiver.

'She's all right, mate,' Marc says. 'You won't get in the way, will you?'

Teish shakes her head from side to side, swallows what's left of her fleeting sadness and her smile rises once again.

'Okay, just don't get in the way.' Kim eyeballs Teish but she just moves a little closer to Marc.

'Has anyone read the assignment questions?'

'Sure did,' Joe answers proudly. 'Who's taking notes?'

'I will,' Marc responds.

'You really are hopeless, even I know how to do this,' Joe looks at Kim. 'I'm the least studious here and even *I* know what to do.'

'I'm not hopeless, I just don't want to do this.

I live in a house with a sister who literally thinks she lives in a Disney movie. As a PRINCESS!'

'I AM a princess!' Teish jumps to her feet.

'Teish! Stop it or go play somewhere else if you can't keep quiet and sit still.'

'Calm down, mate. She's cute, and she might have some of the answers we need. Come and sit here,' Marc says, patting the sofa next to him for her to sit down. 'How are you a princess, Teish?'

'Dad said I am, and he calls Mum his queen, and I am Mum's daughter, and the queen's daughter is a princess, so I must be a princess.'

'Sounds logical,' Marc nods his approval.

'Then I must be a prince,' Kim announces.

Marc laughs and Joe responds, 'Yeah, nah, there's no logic in that.'

Teish stands up with her hands on her hips. 'You cannot be a prince because princes behave better then you do.'

'Burn!' Joe laughs. 'She's got you there, mate.'

Kim is annoyed, looking for something to say. 'Well, well, oh, everyone's a comedian, aren't they? Can we just get started?'

'Yes please,' Teish claps her hands.

Kim presses play on the remote and quickly looks confused. 'What's that say?' Kim asks.

'Gee, the movie hasn't even started, are you going to be asking this for the next hour and a half?' Marc asks.

'Maybe.'

'It's a disclaimer about how their movies of the past have stereotypes and cultural biases, and are racist. I'm writing that in my report,' Marc says.

'I'm bored already,' Joe says, putting his notebook on the ground.

'Shhhh,' Teish orders, not taking her eyes from the screen as the movie finally begins.

'Wow, this is violent for kids,' Marc says.

'And the script is a bit sarcastic too,' Joe adds.

'You're only in trouble if you get caught, now that's a line I'm going to remember,' Kim scribbles in his notebook.

Marc whispers to anyone listening, 'Does anyone else think Aladdin is a little like Robin Hood, you know, stealing that bread then giving it to the poor?'

'He stole it for himself first though, but *he* is poor too,' Teish whispers back.

'Woah,' Joe says loudly. 'Princess Jasmine is hot for a cartoon character. She looks like that girl in year nine, you know the one?'

'Emma?' Kim says.

'Yeah Emma, of course you know her, she lubs you.'

'Don't be ridiculous.'

'Yeah Joe, don't be ridiculous. She'd need to live back in the old days where marriage was arranged by class and not for love, 'cause Emma's never gonna love you.'

'Like Princess Jasmine will never love Jafar,' Teish schools the boys. 'You should marry for love, Marc,' she looks starry-eyed at the teen. 'Women shouldn't have to marry anyone they don't want to.'

'You are absolutely right, Teish.'

Kim scoffs. 'Are you kidding? Women had it easy back then, getting married so that a man could take care of them and provide for them. What a joke.'

Marc looks surprised by his friend's comments. 'Are you kidding? What about freedom?'

'And what are *you* writing down?' Kim asks Joe.

'That this movie for kids has adult themes, there's violence that doesn't have any real consequences, including violence against women, there's adult humour, and I reckon this would scare little kids, don't you?'

'It doesn't scare me, 'cause I'm not that little any more, I turned eight last week.' Teish moves to the television and points to the screen where Princess Jasmine wears teal blue harem pants and a bra top. 'I'm going to wear an outfit like that too one day.'

'Absolutely not! No sister of mine is going to dress like that.'

Marc and Joe start laughing and Teish gets upset.

'What are you laughing at?'

Joe slaps his thigh and says to Kim, 'That monkey Abu is smarter than you.'

'Why?'

'You tell him, Marc.'

'Do you realise how sexist you sound, Kim?'

'And I can wear whatever I want, Kim. You can't tell me how to dress.'

'Yeah, yeah, can we get back to the movie?'

'I wish I had a lamp to rub and a three wishes genie!' Joe starts rubbing his water bottle. 'Maybe this'll work.'

'What would your first wish be?' Kim asks.

Teish looks dreamily at Marc. 'I'd wish for my own Prince Charming.'

'I'd wish for a lifetime supply of hamburgers with the lot!' Joe licks his lips and rubs his stomach at the same time.

'What's going on?' Karan and Ruby walk into the loungeroom, eating ice-cream.

'We're watching Aladdin and pretending we get to wish for something,' Teish waves them in to sit down.

'That's easy,' Ruby declares. 'I wish I make the AFL Women's league.'

'I wish to get the marks and opportunity to be a professor at the best university in the world,' Karan says.

'What about you, Marc?' Teish looks dreamily hoping his wish involves her.

Marc thinks for a second, then nods. 'I wish for the Swans to win every grand final for a decade.' He asks Kim, 'What about you?'

'I wish you'd all shut up talking stupid and let me finish watching this movie! The report is due tomorrow.'

'I need the dyilawa,' Joe says.

'True god, you all make me weak. I need a break, let's take five,' Kim says, and huffs out of the room.

The other boys follow and Teish races to find her mother. When she re-enters the loungeroom the boys are settling in to watch the rest of the film.

'Mum and I made this for you because Kim really likes it.'

The guys laugh, Kim frowns and denies, 'I do not!'

'Yes, you do, I saw you eat a whole plate of fairy bread at my birthday. You *really, really* love it, there was none left for us kids.'

'You really do have a wild imagination, kiddo,'

Kim looks embarrassed that he's been shown up for his childish food fancies and tries to change the subject quickly. 'So, with all that imagination, where would you travel to if you had a magic carpet then?'

'That's easy, Disneyland of course!' Teish tilts her head to suggest it is a no-brainer question. 'And then I would travel to Louisiana to have the best gumbo in the world.'

'Gumbo? Don't you mean jumbo, something?' Kim asks.

'No, I mean gumbo, with a gee. I know you all think the movies I watch are all just pretty girls and frogs that might turn into princes, but they are also about faraway places, cities and new foods too. Gumbo is like a rice stew but really spicy.'

'Maybe you could make roo gumbo—roombo?' Joe says and Teish giggles.

'Where would you ride the magic carpet to?' Teish asks her brother.

'I'd ride the carpet to Hawaii and then ride the best waves in the world at the Pipeline.' He stands up and pretends to be balancing on a surfboard.

Teish turns to her big sister. 'What about you?'

'Well, I'd get that magic carpet to fly back in time where I could sit with the Ancestors and learn all about the stars and astronomy from them. They knew it all before it was in books.'

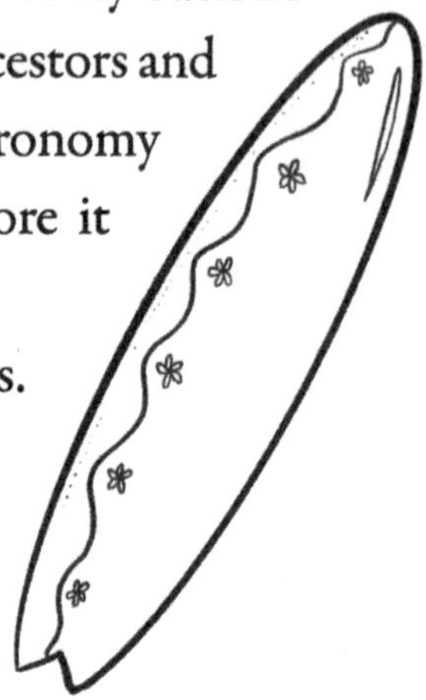

'That'd be so deadly,' Ruby says. 'So, if we could go back in time, I'd go back to when the AFL first started with the mob in Victoria, when Koories called it marngrook and they played with a ball made from possum skin and stuffed with emu feathers.'

'But back then only men played Ruby, so you'd be the first woman then to have a crack at it.'

'Yeah, that'd be even more cool!' Ruby smiles at Marc. 'What about you?' she asks, and Marc is chuffed she is focusing on him.

'Me? I'd ride that carpet as part of the Long Walk into that deadly Dreamtime at the 'G event they do every year, *and* I'd get Michael Long to ride with me.'

'Cool.'

'Wow.'

'Solid.'

'Deadly.'

'And where would the funny guy go?' Teish giggles, referring to Joe.

'I'd ride the carpet back home to my country, to sit with Grandfather. He is the best storyteller ever and has the funniest jokes. He reckons he's a good singer too, will pull out that guitar and do Koorioke anytime, anywhere for anyone. True god, he is the funniest fella you will ever meet.'

'You take after him,' Teish gives Joe a hug.

'I reckon I do, you want me to sing ya a song?'

'NO!' the other teenagers sing out in unison.

'Maybe later,' Teish leans in and whispers to Joe.

Kim suddenly pauses the television.

'What do you see?' he asks.

'A frozen screen?'

'Look harder at the screen, then at me.' The others do as instructed and Kim sits tall, grinning widely.

'What are we supposed to see?' Teish asks.

'I look like Aladdin or, actually, he looks like me.'

'He DOES look like you, Kim. He is brown and good-looking,' Teish says, proud of her handsome brother.

The others roll around on the floor laughing.

'Ah forget it, you mob have no idea,' Kim presses play on the movie again and sulks for the remainder of the film.

FIVE

Trick or treat

'Hold the ladder steady Helen, or you might end up with me falling on top of you.' Jamie is sweating as he strains to hang some fake spider webbing across the front of their home.

'See, Halloween is dangerous. There were quite a few kids that ended up in emergency last year. It's a night I dread as a nurse, and that is no exaggeration.'

'What's that, love?'

'Are you selective hearing me again, James?'

'What's that?' He chuckles until Helen starts

to shake the ladder and giggles a little too. 'Hey, that's not fair! I'm trying to do something nice for the kids of the neighbourhood.'

'Maybe you could watch them cross the road tonight then. I mean it's dangerous with them all roaming the streets. No-one looks left and right anymore, too busy looking for the house with the most junk food to give away. Honestly, I'm surprised no-one got killed last year.'

'You really are a worry wart sometimes, my love.'

Helen shakes her head as Kim appears. 'Son, hold the ladder so your mother can go carve some pumpkins.'

Kim takes the ladder and Helen walks off determined to have the last word. 'We really should be carving emu eggs.'

'Hand me that plastic bat near your feet will you, Son?'

'Why are we celebrating Halloween? Isn't it an American thing, Dad?'

'It's actually an ancient Celtic festival that started two thousand years ago. People would wear costumes and light fires to ward off birig-galang.'

'Kind of like our smoking ceremonies to cleanse negative energy?'

'Maybe back in the day it was more cultural than it is today. I'm sure they weren't collecting chocolates and lollies or dressing up in superhero costumes like they do these days.'

'Is it a Catholic thing then?'

'It's a pagan festival, Son. Now hand me that plastic spider over there.'

'What's a pagan?'

'Someone who believes in alternative religions to the mainstream.'

'I must be a pagan then Dad, if I believe in Biyaami and not a Christian god?'

'Well, I think ...' and before Jamie has a chance to think about a proper answer Kim butts in.

'So, if I'm a pagan then it's okay to celebrate Halloween, right?' A twinkle in his eye suggests Kim has a plan.

*

'Mum, I need a costume for tomorrow too.'

'What?' Ruby says. 'I thought you weren't

buying into all that American consumerism crap.'

'It's pagan consumerism, and I'm a pagan,' Kim says.

'You're a fool,' Karan interjects.

'Stop it, all of you,' Helen says. 'There is no name calling in this house, you know that.' She looks to her husband for backup.

'Your mother is right, and no-one is a pagan or a fool. And you should all have a costume for tomorrow night, you know we do this as a family.'

Karan rolls her eyes.

'And don't do that, it's disrespectful. I am getting tired of telling you.'

Teish bounds into the room. 'I'm going as Pocahontas!'

'Teish, the Powhatan didn't have princesses in their culture, like we don't have princesses in ours.' Helen says.

'But her father was a chief, which is like a king and the daughter of a king is a princess.'

'Then Dad must be a king and I, I must be a prince!' Kim declares as if making an official announcement.

Everyone rolls their eyes and the room erupts with laughter.

*

'Trick or treat?' Kim sings out as he meets everyone outside his home.

Joe looks twice at his mate's costume then laughs. 'Oh, you are hilarious!'

'What? Why?' Kim is confused.

'Your little sister can't be a princess but you can be Aladdin, that's double standards,' Marc explains.

'Guess we should call you the Street Rat instead of the Golden Boy now, eh?' Joe asks.

'Yeah, yeah, I know, but I look like that brother, don't you reckon?' Kim strikes a pose and his mates keel over laughing.

'You really do, Kim. Aladdin is handsome and tall and brown, just like you.' Teish is genuine and enthusiastic in her compliment.

'Who are *they* dressed as?' Kim screws his face up trying to figure out Ruby's and Karan's costumes.

'Karan is Mary Jackson, that Black American lady who was really good at numbers and is famous for helping men get into space.'

'And what about Cuz?' Kim asks.

'Ruby is Kira Phillips.'

'Ruby is beautiful,' Marc says, and the other fellas cringe and nudge each other. 'I mean how beautiful it is that she is paying tribute to the first Aboriginal woman to score a goal in the women's AFL.'

'How do you even know that?' Joe asks.

'You're a freak,' Kim adds.

'Yeah, coming from the guy with the bare chest under the vest he's teamed with a fez and harem pants.' The three burst out laughing.

'What's going on here?' Ruby and Karan join the group and immediately start laughing when they see Kim.

'Well, well, well, how the tide turns for some,' Ruby stands hands on hips, eyeing her cousin up and down.

'Or how the magic carpet flips,' Karan adds.

'You should've drawn some hair on that chest of yours, Cuz.'

'Our own Aladdin, next you'll be Robin Hood, stealing from the rich and giving to the poor, eh Ruby?'

'See, Kim really does like princess movies,' Teish says excitedly.

'No, I don't,' he argues, but on seeing his little sister's lip drop, 'but I *do* like Aladdin!' He rubs Teish's head affectionately.

'Goodes-y, nice choice,' Ruby comments on Marc's outfit, walking around him and checking the number 37 on his guernsey. 'Twice Brownlow medallist. Legend.' Marc stands taller, puffs his chest out as much to impress Ruby as to respect his hero.

'And you?' Karan asks Joe. 'Why are you in a lab coat?'

'I'm Dr Dolittle—the Eddie Murphy version of course, 'cause he's a funny Black man. He's a doctor and he can speak to animals, so the lab coat's for you, Professor.'

Karan seems mildly impressed with Joe's efforts then turns to the group. 'Are we going trick or treating now?'

'I want to stay here and give away the treats I made. Have you had one?' she asks enthusiastically, pushing her bowl towards Karan. 'They're river mint brownies wrapped in recycled wax paper because that's good for the environment,' she adds proudly.

They take one each and devour the treat with moans of tastebud pleasure.

'Yum.'

'Wow.'

'Delicious.'

'Amazing.'

'Can the fresh prince have another one?' Kim presses his hands together and mouths, 'Pretty please?'

'The greedy prince more like it,' Teish giggles as she hands him another wrapped goodie.

'You're very clever, Teish. See, you don't need all this princess stuff,' Karan flicks the tulle on the shoulder of Teish's pink dress.

'I know I don't *need* the princess stuff,' she pushes Karan's hand away, 'but I like it. And I know you all think I am a baby and stupid.'

'No, we don't.'

'I like pink. I like pretty dresses, and I like to dream about nice things. But I don't want to be like one of those characters where the men tell the women who they can marry and who control their freedom. That's not a life for any woman.'

The five teenagers look shocked at their little sister and cousin.

'What? I'm old enough to know that, and I'm smart enough too. And I know you all talk about me, thinking I'm silly loving my princess movies,' she eyeballs them one at a time. 'But I am not a child. I am eight years old. I know you know that because you ate all my fairy bread and birthday cake, and crashed my skipping!' She looks to Ruby. The teenagers don't know where to look.

'And just so you all know: I *do* know the difference between what's real and what is fake. I know kissing frogs won't find me a prince either.'

The teenagers are left speechless as Teish continues.

'You know why I'm dressed like Tiana today?'

The teens are now too scared to answer, feeling suitably chastised by the not-so-childish princess in front of them.

'I'll tell you why! Tiana always dreamed of having her own business, owning her own restaurant and making the best gumbo in Louisiana. I want to own my own shop too, a bakery, making treats for birthdays like I did for my party. Tiana inspired me, that's why I'm dressed like her.'

'That's really cool, kiddo,' Kim says with respect for his baby sister, who he realises is not a baby anymore.

'I know. There's Tiana's Palace in New Orleans. So what about Teish's Bakery in Newcastle?' She looks around for approval from the others. 'Same but different, right?'

The teens smile in acknowledgement.

'Tiana had a dream as a little girl and so do I. And she also had parents who were in love and so do I.' Teish smiles at the thought of her beautiful parents.

'But didn't she also have to kiss a frog?' Karan asks carefully.

'Well, she married a frog when she was a frog too. It's a long story, Karan. You'll have to watch the movie.'

'Okay,' Karan gives in.

'Anyway, I know kissing frogs to turn them into princes isn't real.'

'So you understand that is all fiction and fairytales?'

'Of course, I'm not a baby, I'm eight years old.'

'Phew! Thank goodness! What a relief!'

'If you all spent more time doing things that bring you joy—like me watching princess movies—and less time talking about me pretending to be a princess, then I reckon you'd all be much happier.'

'You've got a point there, kiddo,' Kim says.

'So will you promise to stop talking about me behind my back, when my ears are on the side of my head and I can still hear you? And stop judging me, because Mum told me people who judge others are really just insecure in themselves.'

'Are you sure you're only eight years old?' Marc asks.

'She takes after her cousin, you know,' Ruby puts her arm around Teish.

'Ha, as if!' Karan slides up to the other side of her little sister. 'More like her older sister, isn't it, Teish?'

'I'm not even going to bother,' Kim looks away.

'I take after Mum, she's the queen of our castle,' Teish says, walking off and singing out, 'Trick or treat?'

ABOUT THE AUTHOR

Anita Heiss is a proud Wiradyuri woman who was born on Gadigal Country and spent much of her life on Dharawal land near La Perouse. She is one of Australia's most prolific and well-known authors publishing across genres including non-fiction, historical fiction, commercial fiction and children's novels.

Her children's novels include *Who Am I? The Diary of Mary Talence* (2001), *Harry's Secret* (2015), *Matty's Comeback* (2016), *Kicking Goals with Goodesy and Magic* (2016), co-written with Adam Goodes and Michael O'Loughlin and *Our Race for Reconciliation* (2017). She also wrote two kids' novels with students from La Perouse Public School – *Yirra and Her Deadly Dog Demon* (2007) and *Demon Guards the School Yard* (2011).

Anita loves chocolate, running and summer days at the beach.